Flamingo's Cabin

Llama's Lodge

Yak's Shack

N

W   E

For Libby—M. R.

For Granny Betty—E. F.

First published in paperback in Great Britain by HarperCollins Children's Books in 2017
This edition published in 2017

1 3 5 7 9 10 8 6 4 2

ISBN: 978-0-00-819418-5

HarperCollins Children's Books is a division of HarperCollins Publishers Ltd.

Text copyright © Michelle Robinson 2017
Illustrations copyright © Emily Fox 2017

Visit our website at www.harpercollins.co.uk

Printed in China

MONKEY'S SANDWICH

Michelle Robinson
Illustrated by Emily Fox

HarperCollins *Children's Books*

Monkey's tummy was rumbling.
His breakfast plate was bare.
None of the shops were open yet.
"Perhaps my friends will share . . .?"

"Yak won't mind,"
he told himself.
"She's fast asleep in bed ..."

He sneaked inside
and helped himself
to butter
and some bread.

He tiptoed to the garden bench.

"Just plain old bread? How boring."

In Mouse's house he spied . . .

"Some **cheese!**

(I'd ask first, but he's snoring.)"

A **big**
cheese
sandwich

—just the thing!
BUT Monkey
wanted more.

He left a hasty
"Thank You" note
and took a look
next door.

Elephant had some **cucumber.**

DonKey had some custard.

Flamingo had some **jellybeans,** some **chocolate spread**

... and mustard.

Monkey stacked them up,
then licked his lips
and started yawning.
He'd never made a sandwich
quite so early in the morning.

He added berries

(several kinds),

some pizza,

and bananas.

Monkey's sandwich
GREW
and
GREW.

Next stop:
the fridge at Llama's.

At one point Monkey
wondered if he'd been
a trifle selfish ...
But then he spotted

soft
whipped
cream,

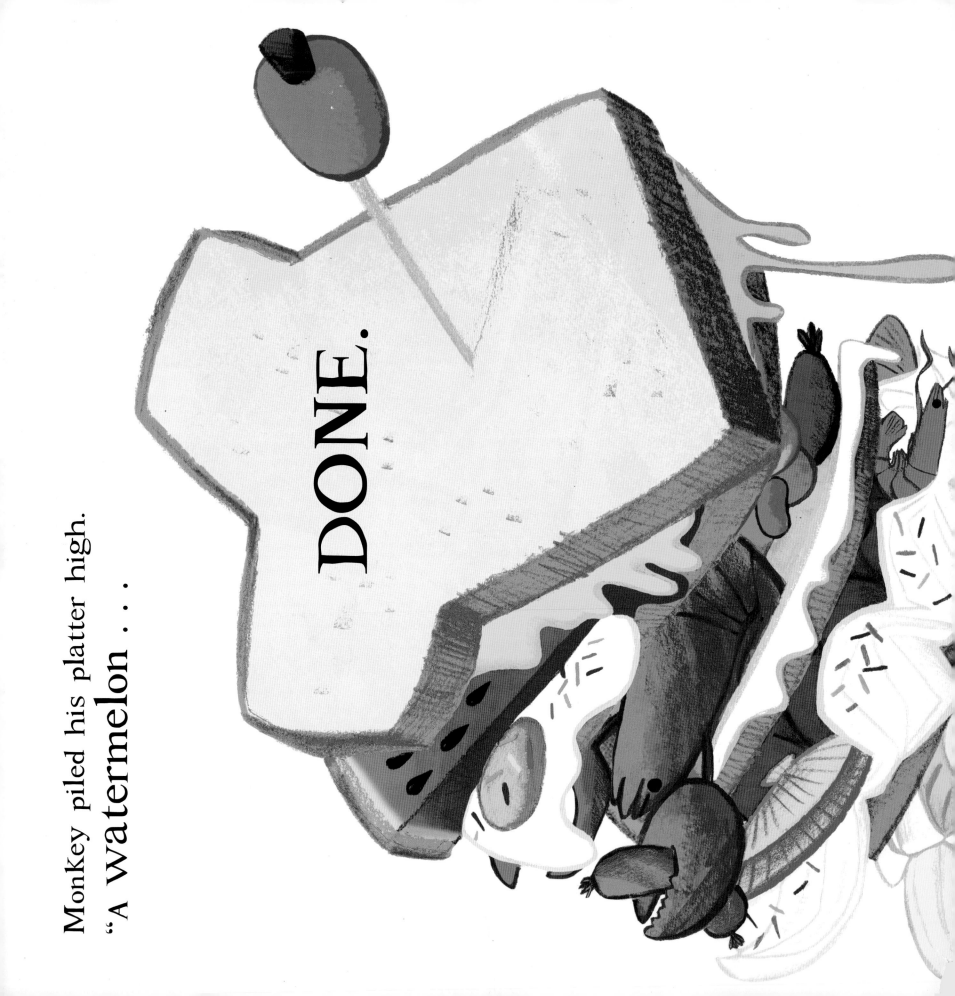

Monkey piled his platter high. "A watermelon . . . .

DONE.

One super sandwich
coming up."
Just like the
rising sun . . .

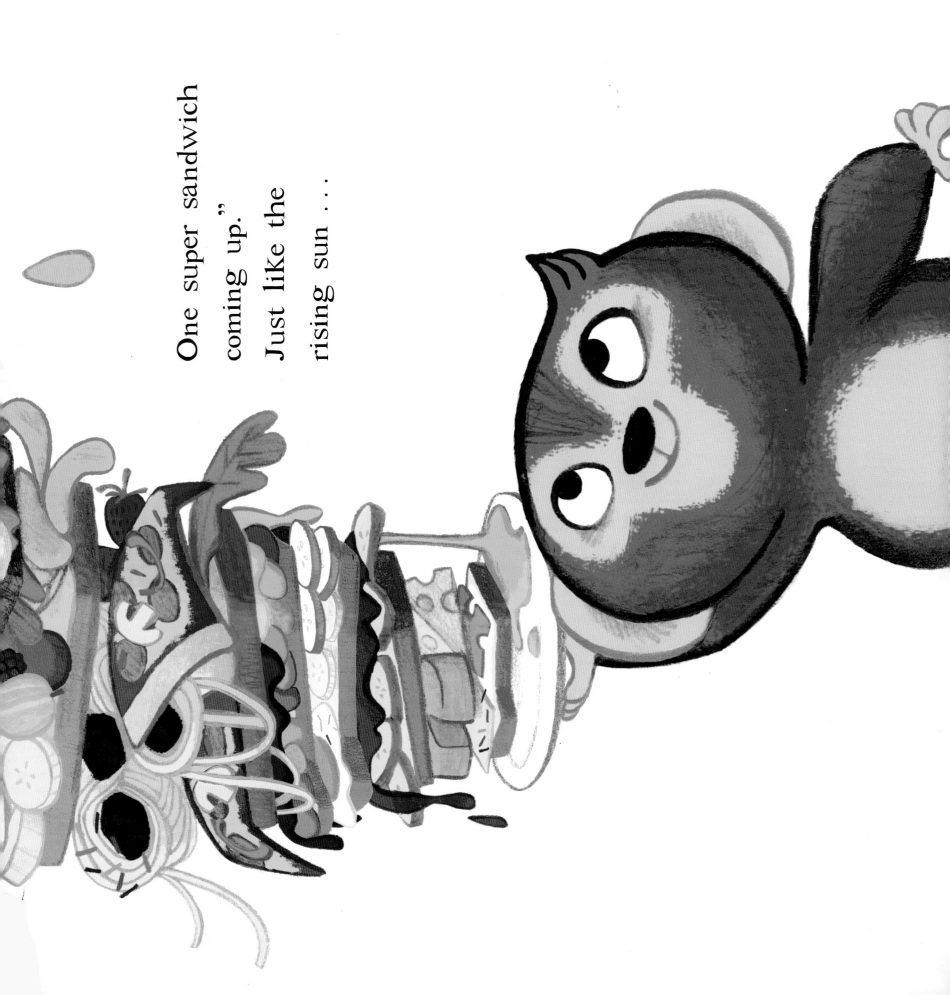

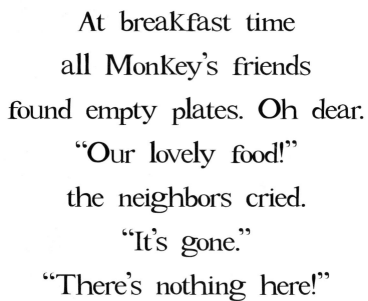

At breakfast time
all Monkey's friends
found empty plates. Oh dear.
"Our lovely food!"
the neighbors cried.
"It's gone."
"There's nothing here!"

"A thief!" said Donkey. "Follow me,
I'm sure we'll find a clue."

"Ahem," squeaked Mouse.
"I found a note—from Monkey.
Will this do?"

I took your cheese—
thanks, Monkey

The friends rushed
round to Monkey's house.

"You cheeky chimp."
"How rude."
"You can't just go round
tucking into someone else's food."

But Monkey was exhausted
and he'd gone straight back to bed.
The evidence was still intact.
"Looks tasty," Llama said.

Monkey's sandwich.
What a feast! Enough for everyone.
And sharing all their favorite things
was really rather fun.

"Perhaps," said Mouse, "we ought to save our friend a slice or two?"
They also left him something else . . .

A shopping list to do.

Elephant's Estate

Donkey's Tepee

Monkey's Hut

Mouse's House